Oh, the THINKS you Can Think!

想怎麼想 就怎麼想

by Dr. Seuss

文・圖　蘇斯博士
譯　　郝廣才

想怎麼想就怎麼想　　　　　　　　　　　　　　　　蘇斯博士小孩學讀書全集 9

發行／1992 年 12 月 25 日初版 1 刷　1994 年 6 月 25 日初版 3 刷

著／蘇斯博士

譯／郝廣才

責任編輯／郝廣才　張玲玲　劉思源

美術編輯／李純真　郭倖惠　陳素芳

發行人／王榮文　出版者／遠流出版事業股份有限公司　台北市汀州路 3 段 184 號 7 F 之 5

行政院新聞局局版臺業字第 1295 號　郵撥／0189456-1　電話／（02）365-3707　傳真／（02）365-7979

印刷／Wing Yiu Printing Co.

ISBN 957 - 32 - 1427 - X　　　　　　　　　　　　　　　　　　　　　　　　　NT$185

You can
think up
some birds.

That's what you can do.
You can think about yellow
or think about blue...

你³ˇ可ㄎㄜˇ以ㄧˇ
想ㄒㄧㄤˇ像ㄒㄧㄤ
一ㄧ些ㄒㄧㄝ鳥ㄋㄧㄠˇ，
你³ˇ可ㄎㄜˇ以ㄧˇ做ㄗㄨㄛ得ㄉㄜ到ㄉㄠˋ。
想ㄒㄧㄤˇ想ㄒㄧㄤˇ黃ㄏㄨㄤ的ㄉㄜ鳥ㄋㄧㄠˇ
身ㄕㄣ上ㄕㄤ穿ㄔㄨㄢ著ㄓㄜ藍ㄌㄢ外ㄨㄞ套ㄊㄠˋ……

You can think about red.
You can think about pink.
You can think up a horse.
Oh, the THINKS you can think!

你ふ可ぇ以ˇ想ぇ紅ら，
可ぇ以ˇ想ぇ粉ふ紅ら。
想ぇ啊ぐ想ぇ，　想ぇ不ふ停ぇ，
想ぇ一一匹ぇ馬ふ在ぇ其ふ中き。

Oh, the THINKS
you can think up
if only you try!
If you try,
you can think up
a GUFF going by.

發揮你的想像力，
只要你努力。
只要你努力，
你可以想像
一隻毛球走過草地。

And you don't have to stop.
You can think about SCHLOPP.
Schlopp. Schlopp. Beautiful schlopp.
Beautiful schlopp
with a cherry on top.

不要停，快動腦，
想像一個超派糕。
超派糕，超派糕，
美麗的超派糕，
上面有櫻桃。

You can think about gloves.
You can think about SNUVS.

可²以ˇ想ˇ手ˇ套ˋ，

可²以ˇ想ˇ草ˇ貓¹，

You can think a long time
about snuvs and their gloves.

想_{ㄒㄧㄤˇ}想_{ㄒㄧㄤˇ}草_{ㄘㄠˇ}貓_{ㄇㄠ}加_{ㄐㄧㄚ}手_{ㄕㄡˇ}套_{ㄊㄠˋ}，
花_{ㄏㄨㄚ}的_{ㄉㄜ˙}時_{ㄕˊ}間_{ㄐㄧㄢ}可_{ㄎㄜˇ}不_{ㄅㄨˋ}少_{ㄕㄠˇ}。

You can think about
Kitty O'Sullivan Krauss
in her big balloon swimming pool
over her house.

想想凱蒂沙利文克勞茲
在她的超級吹氣游泳池
跳水的樣子。

Think of black water.
Think up a white sky.
Think up a boat.
Think of BLOOGS blowing by.

想想黑的水，
想想白的天，
一隻小船在中間，
充氣魚，飛滿天。

You can think about Night,
a night in Na-Nupp.
The birds are asleep
and the three moons are up.

你ㄋㄧˇ可ㄎㄜˇ以ㄧˇ想ㄒㄧㄤˇ想ㄒㄧㄤˇ晚ㄨㄢˇ上ㄕㄤˋ，
在ㄗㄞˋ樓ㄌㄡˊ上ㄕㄤˋ樓ㄌㄡˊ的ㄉㄜ˙晚ㄨㄢˇ上ㄕㄤˋ。
鳥ㄋㄧㄠˇ兒ㄦˊ都ㄉㄡ進ㄐㄧㄣˋ入ㄖㄨˋ夢ㄇㄥˋ鄉ㄒㄧㄤ，
天ㄊㄧㄢ上ㄕㄤˋ有ㄧㄡˇ三ㄙㄢ個ㄍㄜˋ月ㄩㄝˋ亮ㄌㄧㄤˋ。

You can think about Day,
a day in Da-Dake.
The water is blue
and the birds are awake.

天_{ㄊㄧㄢ}外_{ㄨㄞ}天_{ㄊㄧㄢ}，　想_{ㄒㄧㄤ}白_{ㄅㄞ}天_{ㄊㄧㄢ}。

鳥_{ㄋㄧㄠ}兒_ㄦ清_{ㄑㄧㄥ}醒_{ㄒㄧㄥ}，　海_{ㄏㄞ}水_{ㄕㄨㄟ}正_{ㄓㄥ}藍_{ㄌㄢ}。

Think! Think and wonder.
Wonder and think.
How much water
can fifty-five elephants drink?

想問題，　心懷疑。
大象五十五頭
要喝多少水才夠？

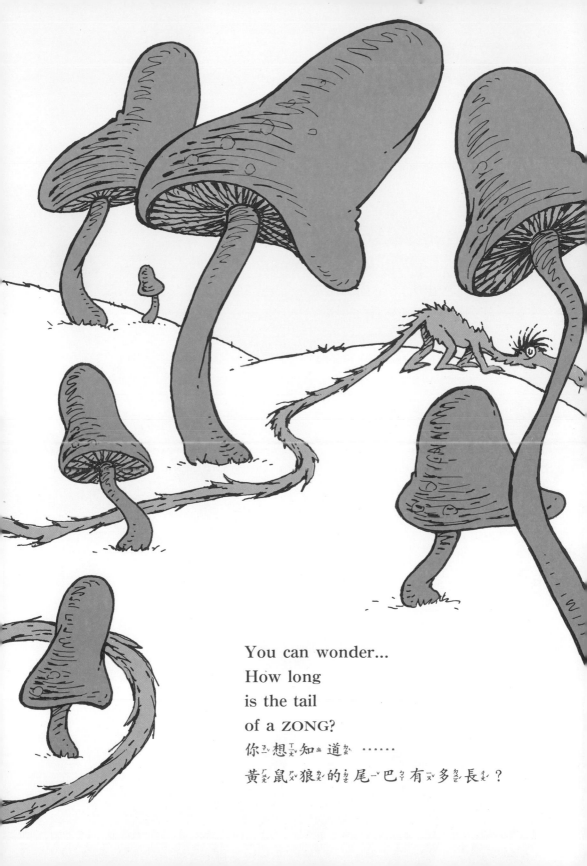

You can wonder...
How long
is the tail
of a ZONG?
你²想¹知ⁱ道⁴ ……
黃²鼠³狼²的⁵尾¹巴¹有³多²長²？

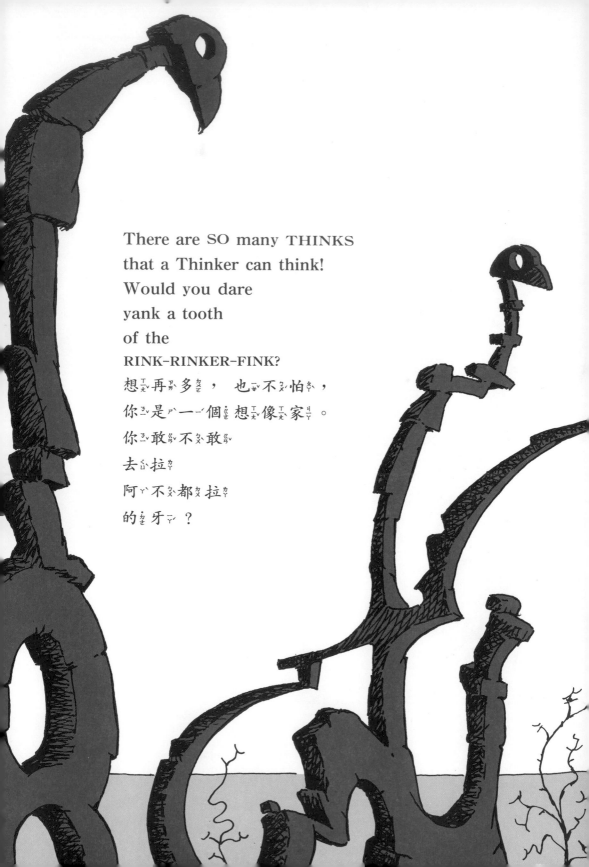

There are SO many THINKS
that a Thinker can think!
Would you dare
yank a tooth
of the
RINK-RINKER-FINK?
想再多，也不怕，
你是一個想像家。
你敢不敢
去拉
阿不都拉
的牙？

And
what would
you do
if
you met
a JIBBOO?
如果你
碰到黑哥，
你會做什麼？

Oh, the THINKS
you can think!

哦ㄜ， 愛ㄞˋ怎ㄗㄣˇ麼ㄇㄜ想ㄒㄧㄤˇ
就ㄐㄧㄡˋ怎ㄗㄣˇ麼ㄇㄜ想ㄒㄧㄤˇ！

Think of
Peter the Postman
who crosses the ice
once every day —
and on Saturdays, twice.

郵差彼得跑得快，
天天滑過大冰塊。
星期六，他也來，
一天兩次不例外。

THINK! You can think
any THINK
that you wish...
想ㄒ一ㄤˇ！ 愛ㄞˋ怎ㄗㄣˇ麼ㄇㄜ˙想ㄒ一ㄤˇ
就ㄐ一ㄡˋ怎ㄗㄣˇ麼ㄇㄜ˙想ㄒ一ㄤˇ ……

Think
a race
on a horse
on a ball
with a fish!

騎ㄑㄧˊ馬ㄇㄚˇ滾ㄍㄨㄣˇ球ㄑㄧㄡˊ，
頭ㄊㄡˊ頂ㄉㄧㄥˇ魚ㄩˊ，
瘋ㄈㄥ狂ㄎㄨㄤˊ賽ㄙㄞˋ馬ㄇㄚˇ
真ㄓㄣ有ㄧㄡˇ趣ㄑㄩˋ！

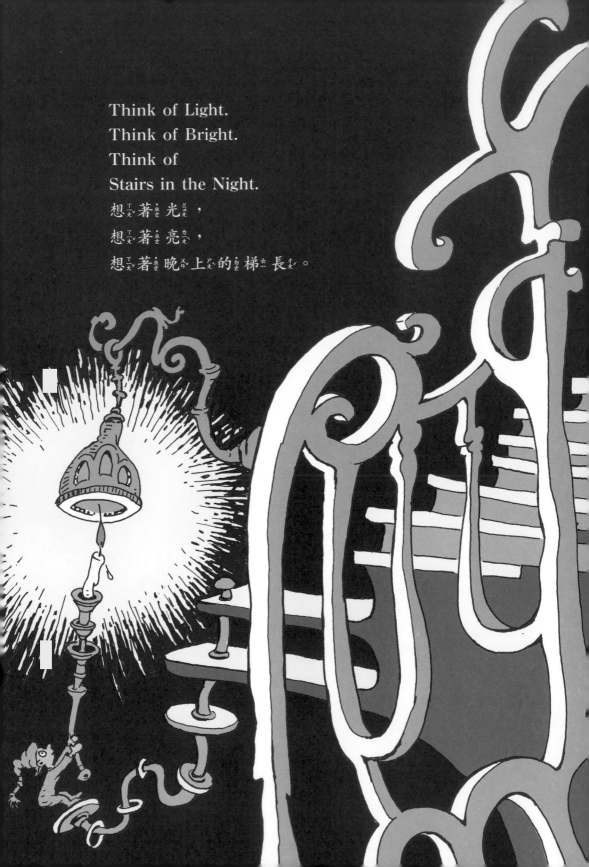

Think of Light.
Think of Bright.
Think of
Stairs in the Night.
想著光，
想著亮，
想著晚上的梯長。

THINK!

Think a ship.

Think up a long trip.

Go visit the VIPPER, the Vipper of Vipp.

我要駕著小艇，

展開長途旅行。

去到天堂島，拜訪天堂鳥。

And left!
Think of Left!
還ㄏㄞ有ㄧㄡˇ左ㄗㄨㄛˇ邊ㄅㄧㄢ，
想ㄒㄧㄤˇ想ㄒㄧㄤˇ左ㄗㄨㄛˇ邊ㄅㄧㄢ！

And think about BEFT.
Why is it that beft
always go to the left?
為ㄨㄟˊ什ㄕㄣˊ麼ㄇㄜ˙十ㄕˊ八ㄅㄚ羅ㄌㄨㄛˊ漢ㄏㄢˋ雞ㄐㄧ
總ㄗㄨㄥˇ是ㄕˋ走ㄗㄡˇ到ㄉㄠˋ左ㄗㄨㄛˇ邊ㄅㄧㄢ去ㄑㄩˋ？

And why is it so many things
go to the Right?
You can think about THAT
until Saturday night.

為什麼那麼多東西
通通走到右邊去？
你可以想、想、想、
一直想到星期六的晚上。

Think left and think right
and think low and think high.
Oh, the THINKS you can think up if only you try!

想_{ㄒㄧㄤˇ}左_{ㄗㄨㄛˇ}想_{ㄒㄧㄤˇ}右_{ㄧㄡˋ}想_{ㄒㄧㄤˇ}高_{ㄍㄠ}想_{ㄒㄧㄤˇ}低_{ㄉㄧ}。
哦_{ㄜˊ}，只_{ㄓˇ}要_{ㄧㄠˋ}你_{ㄋㄧˇ}願_{ㄩㄢˋ}意_{ㄧˋ}試_{ㄕˋ}
想_{ㄒㄧㄤˇ}怎_{ㄗㄣˇ}麼_{ㄇㄜ˙}想_{ㄒㄧㄤˇ}就_{ㄐㄧㄡˋ}怎_{ㄗㄣˇ}麼_{ㄇㄜ˙}想_{ㄒㄧㄤˇ}！